MUTT DOG!

For all scruffy Mutts.

S.M.K.

Scholastic Children's Books
Commonwealth House, 1-19 New Oxford Street
London WCIA INU, UK
a division of Scholastic Ltd
London~New York~Toronto~Sydney~Auckland
Mexico City~New Delhi~Hong Kong

First published in Australia by Scholastic Australia Pty Limited, 2004
First published in paperback in the UK by Scholastic Ltd, 2005

Text and illustrations copyright © Stephen Michael King, 2004

ISBN 0 439 954495

Printed in Singapore

2 4 6 8 10 9 7 5 3 1

The right of Stephen Michael King to be identified as the author and illustrator of this
work has been asserted by him in accordance with
the Copyright, Designs and Patents Act, 1988.

Other books by
STEPHEN MICHAEL KING:

WORDS AND PICTURES:

The Man Who Loved Boxes
Patricia
Henry and Amy
Emily Loves to Bounce
Milli, Jack and the Dancing Cat

PICTURES:

Beetle Soup
The Little Blue Parcel
Amelia Ellicott's Garden
Pocket Dogs
Where Does Thursday Go?
Piglet and Mama

Thanks to Trish, Tanith, Luka, Muttley Christmas, Milli, Peppermint, Coco, Margaret Connolly, Margrete Lamond and my sister Mel.

MUTT

WORDS AND PICTURES Stephen Michael King

DOG!

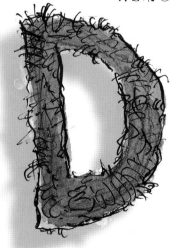

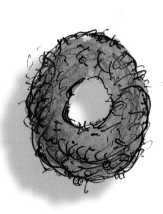

Hippo

In the city lived a dog . . .

who belonged to no-one.

He had to be brave,

and fast,

and smart . . .

just to survive.

He ate whatever he could find.

And looked for a new place to sleep . . .

every night.

One evening he found a halfway house.

Inside there were people

who were cold

and tired . . .

like him.

There wasn't enough room . . .
or even enough food for a dog.

A lady who worked there
tried to put him outside,

but the scruffy dog
wiggled free . . .

and hid in a corner.

What am I going to do with you?

She gave him a biscuit . . .

and made him a bed.

The next morning,
he was on his way. . .

This is no place
for a stray dog.

I wish you
could stay.

The sky was black and his stomach felt empty.

He looked for breakfast,

and a new place to sleep.

'Wait! Scruffy dog!'
called a voice.

It was the lady from
the halfway house.

Would you like
to come home
with me?

They left the city, and the air filled with new smells.

His new family gave him the first bath he'd ever had.

They brushed out
his matted knots,

gave him food from
a big tin can . . .

and something
delicious to chew.

Everyone thought up all sorts
of names —

Bear,

Winston,

Tyrone,

Radiator,

Piccasso,

Fly,

Sigmund,

Heathcliff,

Errol,

Dingo,

Splot,

Dustin,

Affro,

Dredd!

But most of the time everyone called him . . .

Mutt Dog!

Who's a
lucky little
Mutt Dog?

Mutt Dog
is brave,

and fast,

and smart.

He's gentle and loyal,

and each night when he goes to sleep . . .

he knows where he belongs.